W9-DBA-126

SCHOOL SIDEKICKS
FIELD TRIP TROUBLE

by Molly Beth Griffin

illustrated by Mike Deas

PICTURE WINDOW BOOKS
a capstone imprint

TABLE OF CONTENTS

SCHOOL SIDEKICKS

These five friends live within the walls, nooks, and crannies of an elementary school. They learn alongside kids every day, even though the kids don't see them!

STELLA

Stella is a mouse. She loves her friends. She also loves children and school! She came into the school on a cold winter day. She knew it would be her home forever. Her favorite subjects are social studies and music. She is always excited for a new day.

BO

Bo is a parakeet. He is a classroom pet. The friends let him out of his cage so they can play together. Bo loves to read. He goes home with his teacher on weekends, but he always comes back to school to see his friends.

DELILAH

Delilah is a spider. She has always lived in the corners of the school. She is so small the children never notice her, but she is very smart. Delilah loves math and computers and hates the broom.

NICO

Nico is a toad. He used to be a classroom pet. A child forgot to put him back into his tank one day. Now he lives with his friends. The whole school is his home! He can be grumpy, but he loves science and art. Since Nico doesn't have fingers, he paints with his toes!

GOLDIE

Goldie is a goldfish. She is very wise. The friends ask her questions when they have a big choice to make. She gives good advice and lives in the media center.

PAINTER'S BLOCK

Nico the Toad stared at his blank paper for a long time. Then he threw his brush on the floor.

"I give up!" he shouted. "I'm done painting forever!"

"What's wrong?" asked Stella the Mouse.

"Are you hurt?" asked Delilah the Spider.

"Can we help?" asked Bo the Parakeet.

"I don't know what to paint," Nico said. "This has never happened to me before! What should I do?"

He looked like he was going to cry. The friends did not know how to help him.

Then the bell rang. The children thundered through the halls. Stella and her friends leapt out of the way. They hid till the stampede was over.

When they came out, a piece of paper floated down to them. Nico grabbed it out of the air.

"What is it?" they all asked.

Nico held it up as Bo read.

"Field trip at the art museum,"

he said.

"Yes, yes, yes!" said Nico.

"No, no, no," said his friends.

"Looking at lots of beautiful art will be just what I need," said Nico. "It will help me start painting again!"

"But Nico, we can't leave the school," said Stella. "We are safe and warm here. There is food. We are together."

"She's right," said Delilah. "We can't risk getting lost. Or separated. You understand—right, Nico?"

Nico did not understand.

"Let's go ask Goldie," said Bo.

Whenever the friends had a big question, they asked Goldie. She lived in the media center. She was very wise.

"Let's go!" said Nico.

"Goldie, should we go on the field trip to the art museum?" asked Nico.

Goldie swam in a circle.

"Blub," she said.

One blub meant "yes," and two blubs meant "no." At least, that's what the friends thought she meant.

"Yes?" asked Stella. "Did you say yes?"

She could not believe it. Goldie
was very wise. This choice did not
seem wise at all.

"But it's so risky. How will we
get home safe?" asked Delilah.
Goldie looked from Stella to
Nico. Then to Delilah. Then to Bo.
Then back to Stella again.

"Of course!" Stella squeaked. "We can stick together. If we use the buddy system, we'll be okay."

"Thanks, Goldie!" Bo said.

"You always know what to do," Delilah said.

Chapter 2

THE BUDDY SYSTEM

The morning of the field trip, the friends snuck out the front doors of the school. They climbed onto the big yellow bus.

The animal friends hid beneath a seat. They were scared. They were excited too.

"Be sure to stay together and keep track of time. We cannot miss the bus. We'd never get back home again," Stella said.

But once they were inside the museum, their plans quickly fell apart.

Nico hopped away and found the abstract art. He was in awe!

Bo fluttered away and found
the gift shop. It was full of books.

Delilah scurried away and
found the huge marble staircase.

Stella could not keep track of everyone, and it was getting late!

Stella's friends were nowhere to be found. They did not stick together. They did not keep track of time. Would they be left behind?

"What am I going to do?" Stella said.

The children headed back to the bus. Stella had to act fast. She made a brave decision. She took a big risk.

Stella scurried out in the open. She let herself be seen.

Chapter 3

TOGETHER AGAIN

"MOUSE!" cried a man.

"MOUSE!" cried a child.

"MOUSE! MOUSE! MOUSE!"
echoed through the museum.

Stella dashed out of sight
again. Then she reappeared
in a different spot.

"Mouse?" said
Nico. He was still in
the abstract art wing.

"Mouse?" said Bo. He was still
in the gift shop.

"Mouse?" said Delilah. She was
still on the marble staircase.

"Stella!" they all cried, and they came running.

Stella dodged the museum guard. She scuttled away from the janitor's broom.

She herded her friends back onto the bus just before the doors folded shut.

The children were so noisy nobody noticed the little animals at the back of the bus.

They were safe. They were together. And they were headed back to school. Stella sighed. She was quite tired.

"That was scary," she said.

"That was fantastic!" said Nico.

He hopped over to the window. He drew pictures on the foggy glass the whole way back to school.

Nico could not wait to get painting again!

EMERGENCY DOOR

TALK ABOUT IT

1. Stella and her friends feel safe at school. What makes you feel safe?

2. Nico is frustrated when he can't figure out what to paint. Talk about a time you were frustrated. What did you do to make things better?

3. Stella made a brave move to save her friends. Would you have done the same thing?

WRITE ABOUT IT

1. When Nico feels sad, his friends want to cheer him up. Make a list of things you can do to make someone feel better when they are sad.

2. Write about your favorite field trip. Then draw a picture to go with your story.

3. Nico's hobby is painting. Write about your favorite hobby.

MOLLY BETH GRIFFIN

Molly Beth Griffin is a writing teacher at the Loft Literary Center in Minneapolis, Minnesota. She has written numerous picture books (including *Loon Baby* and *Rhoda's Rock Hunt*) and a YA novel *(Silhouette of a Sparrow)*. Molly loves reading and hiking in all kinds of weather. She lives in South Minneapolis with her partner and two kids.

MIKE DEAS

Mike Deas is a cartoonist, illustrator, and graphic novelist. His love for illustrative storytelling comes from an early love of reading and drawing. Capilano College's Commercial Animation Program in Vancouver helped Mike fine-tune his drawing skills and imagination. Mike lives with his family on sunny Salt Spring Island, British Columbia, Canada.

PLENTY OF SIDEKICK FUN!

School Sidekicks is published by
Picture Window Books, a Capstone imprint
1710 Roe Crest Drive, North Mankato, Minnesota 56003
www.capstonepub.com

Library of Congress Cataloging-in-Publication Data
is available on the Library of Congress website.

ISBN: 978-1-5158-4416-7 (library binding)
ISBN: 978-1-5158-4420-4 (ebook pdf)

Summary: Nico the Toad is always a little grumpy. But lately
he's been grumpier than ever. Stella the Mouse, Delilah the Spider,
and Bo the Parakeet think the field trip to the art museum will cheer
him up. But the animal friends have never left the school before.
If they stick together, nothing can go wrong—can it?

Book design by: Ted Williams

Design Elements: Shutterstock: AVA Bitter, Oleksandr Rybitskiy

Printed and bound in the United States of America.
PA71